W9-DFZ-424

3087

818
MAE   Maestro, Giulio

Macho nacho and
other rhyming
riddles

DUE DATE	BRODART	06/98	12.99

Library of Congress Cataloging-in-Publication Data
Maestro, Giulio.   Macho nacho and other rhyming riddles/
by Giulio Maestro.—1st ed.   p. cm.   ISBN 0-525-45261-3
1. Riddles, Juvenile.   [1. Riddles.   2. Jokes.]   I. Title.
PN6371.5.M273   1994   818'.5402—dc20
93-47137   CIP   AC

Published in the United States by Dutton Children's Books,
a division of Penguin Books USA Inc.
375 Hudson Street, New York, New York 10014
Designed by Adrian Leichter
Printed in Hong Kong
First Edition
10 9 8 7 6 5 4 3 2 1

MACHO NACHO

Where does a nacho swim?
In chip dip.

What do you call a he-man tortilla chip?
A macho nacho.

What are musicians on a beach?
A sand band.

How do you plant seeds?
Sow a row.

How do you ask for tiny green vegetables?
"Peas, please?"

What is a flower that won't open?
A dud bud.

How do you catch a taxi?
Grab a cab.

How does an elephant take a shower?
With its hose nose.

How do you educate a fuzzy fruit?
Teach a peach.

What do you call a lunar lullaby?
A moon croon.

What is a stretched-out serenade?
A long song.

Where do you find a police officer's hat?
Atop a cop.

What do you call a gangster's loot?
A hood's goods.

What is a prison for slugs?
A snail jail.

What are Robert's tears?
Bob's sobs.

What is a happy ending for a lost dog?
The hound is found.

What do you call a bunch of bees
in the sun?
A warm swarm.

What is a sweet rabbit?
A honey bunny.

What is truly a dinner?
A real meal.

What does moonlight make?
The night bright.

What do you call a sword fight over
a sapphire?
A jewel duel.

What is a hero's greeting?
A brave wave.

How do you cruise around a castle?
By moat boat.

What do fish do to a pelican's beak?
Fill the bill.

What do you call a swine's dance?
A pig jig.

What did the egg laugh at?
A yolk joke.

What is rosy lemonade?
A pink drink.

What is another name for candy?
A sweet treat.

What do you call a perfect peppermint?
A dandy candy.

Why can't cows keep a secret?
Cattle tattle.

How does a cow cry?
Moo-boo-hoo.

Why did the bull give the cow a valentine?
He was a mooer wooer.

What made one clock run faster than the other?

A quicker ticker.

What do hugging snakes look like?
A tight sight.

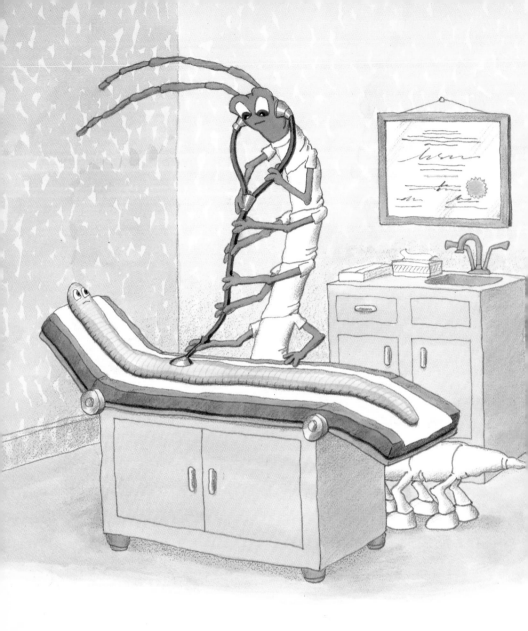

What made the night crawler sick?
A worm germ.

What is spooky breakfast bread?
Ghost toast.

Who sneaks saltines between meals?
A cracker snacker.

What is another name for butter?
Bread spread.

What do you call pasta for pooches?

Noodles for poodles.

How do you prune a tree?
Trim a limb.

How did the car get a dent?
In a fender bender.

Who puts ducks into boxes?
A quacker packer.

What comes after a May melody?
A June tune.

What do cattle eat?
Cow chow.

What is a small snack?
A light bite.

What is licorice eaten between meals?
A black snack.

How do you make a gherkin giggle?
Tickle the pickle.

What is a hairpiece for a hog?
A pig wig.

What do you call a light-colored horse?
A fair mare.

What do you call a damp dog doctor?
A wet vet.

What is the baying of a beagle?
A hound sound.

Where does a grizzly live?
In a bear lair.

What do you call stolen overshoes?
Boot loot.

What do you put in running shoes?
Fleet feet.

What do you call a rock in winter?
A colder boulder.

Where can you take a cold swim?
In a cool pool.

How did the reptiles storm into town?

In a lizard blizzard.

Which athlete has a hard serve?
A tennis menace.

What do you call a quick game?
A short sport.

How do you stray far away?
Wander yonder.

Why did the hen sit on her eggs?
To hatch a batch.

How do you say farewell to a fruit tart?
"Bye-bye, pie!"

HINKY PINKY

A RHYMING RIDDLE GAME

The type of riddles in this book can make a fun game that you can play with one friend or a whole group. To play Hinky Pinky, first think of two words that rhyme, like "mouse house" or "funny money," but don't tell anyone what they are. The object of the game is for everyone else to guess your words. To help them guess, you give two clues. The first is a description clue.

Think of words that describe your two secret words. Your description does not have to rhyme. For instance, if your secret words are "mouse house," then you can describe them by asking your friends, "What do you call a *rodent's home*?"

Your second clue is a syllable clue. Figure out how many syllables are in each of your secret words. If each word has only one syllable, as in "mouse house," you call out "hink pink." This tells everyone that your words have one syllable each. If your secret words have two syllables each, like "funny money," then you say "hinky pinky." If they have three syllables each, like "mystery history," you say "hinkety pinkety." However, your secret words do not have to have the same number of syllables each. If one word has three syllables and the other has two, like "amazing grazing," you say "hinkety pinky."

With a description clue and a syllable clue, your friends can try to guess your secret words. The first person to guess gets to choose the next pair of words. Have fun!